THE PRINCESS
WHO LOST HER HAIR

Library of Congress Cataloging-in-Publication Data

Mollel, Tololwa M. (Tololwa Marti)
    The princess who lost her hair: an Akamba legend / retold by
Tololwa M. Mollel; illustrated by Charles Reasoner.
        p.   cm.—(Legends of the world)
    Summary: The efforts of a kind-hearted beggar boy bring an end to
the drought that has plagued the kingdom of a haughty princess.
    ISBN 0-8167-2815-1 (lib. bdg.)   ISBN 0-8167-2816-X (pbk.)
    [1. Folklore, Kamba (African people) 2. Folklore—Africa, East.]
I. Reasoner, Charles, ill.   II. Title.   III. Series.
PZ8.1.M73Pr 1993
398.21—dc20   92-13273

THE PRINCESS WHO LOST HER HAIR

AN AKAMBA LEGEND

RETOLD BY TOLOLWA M. MOLLEL   ILLUSTRATED BY CHARLES REASONER

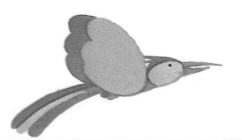

TROLL ASSOCIATES

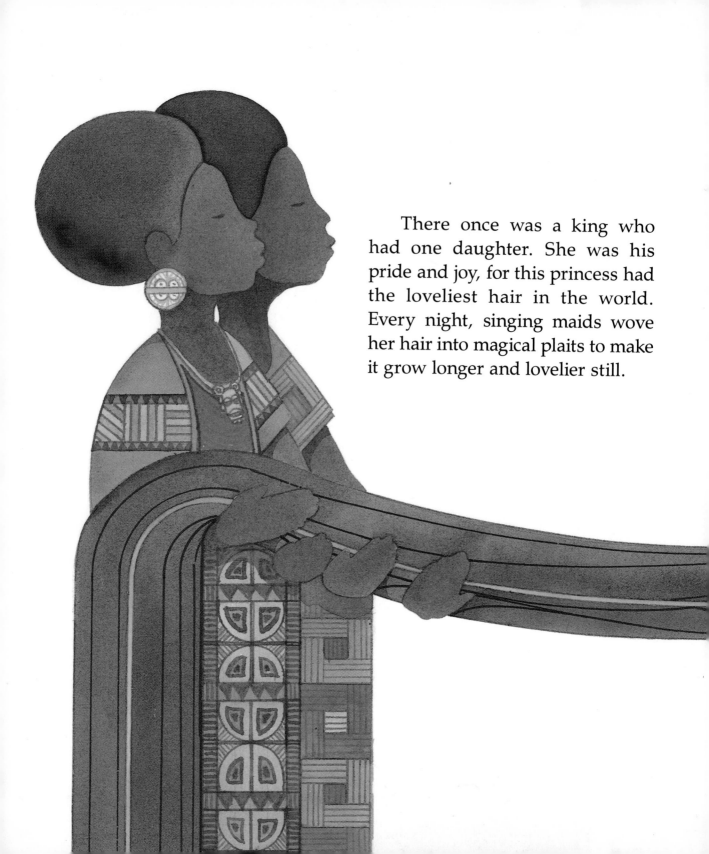

There once was a king who had one daughter. She was his pride and joy, for this princess had the loveliest hair in the world. Every night, singing maids wove her hair into magical plaits to make it grow longer and lovelier still.

Each morning, with the plaits undone and her hair adorned with gold, her handmaidens held her hair up off the ground as the princess strolled from the palace to be admired by her subjects.

NE DAY, as the maids were tending the princess's hair, a large bird landed on the garden wall.

"Good morning, princess," smiled the bird. "I've heard so much about your hair that I had to see it for myself. It is more beautiful than I imagined. It looks so fine and soft, perhaps you could spare a few strands so that I might line my nest?"

The princess was furious. "My beautiful hair for your nest? How dare you suggest such a thing?" she cried.

"Just a little would be enough," the bird replied.

"I love my hair too much to give it to you!"

"You would do well to give me some," warned the bird.

"Go away!" snapped the princess.

"Is that your final word?"

"Yes," shouted the princess. "Now off you go, before I set the soldiers on you!"

"I will go," declared the bird. "But, one day, you'll wish you had been kinder to me. Beware the coming of the dry season, for as the leaves fall, so shall your hair."

The princess and her handmaidens watched in disbelief as the bird flew away. "It's just a foolish, jealous bird," comforted the maids. The princess smiled at their words and joined them in a cheerful song, the bird all but forgotten.

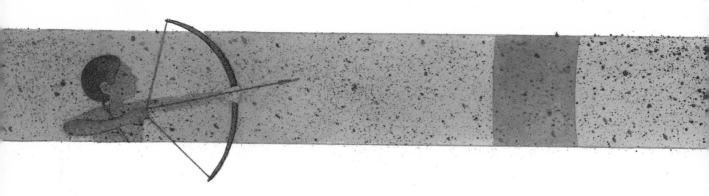

Muoma, a hungry beggar boy, had observed the incident. As he watched the bird fly off, he thought, "I wish I had an arrow. What a fine meal that bird would make!"

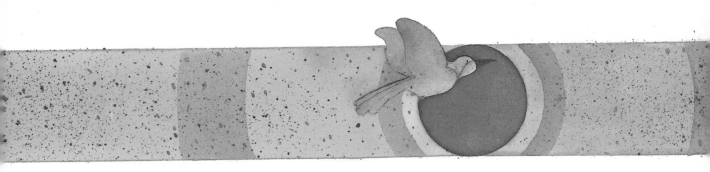

That night, Muoma dreamt of the bird. In his dream, he had a bow and arrow, but the bird flew off before he could shoot it. It disappeared into a blood red sunset, over mountains and plains marked by a lonely path. For many nights, the dream visited him, and each night the bird flew into the sunset.

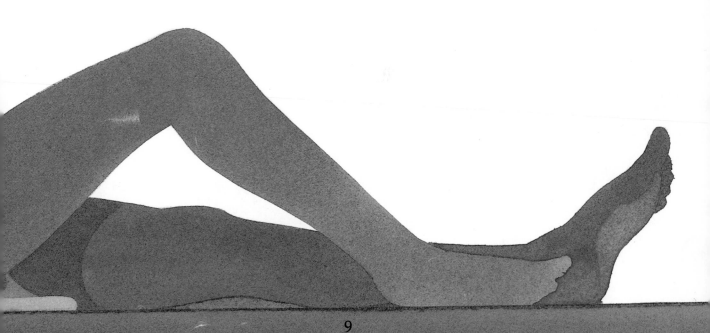

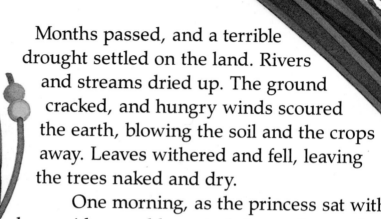

Months passed, and a terrible
drought settled on the land. Rivers
and streams dried up. The ground
cracked, and hungry winds scoured
the earth, blowing the soil and the crops
away. Leaves withered and fell, leaving
the trees naked and dry.

One morning, as the princess sat with
her maids, a sudden wind churned up a thick
cloud of dust. When the dust lifted, the maids
stared in horror at the princess.

"Your hair!" they gasped. "It's gone!" High
in the sky, the princess's hair twisted out of sight in
the grip of the powerful wind. With a shriek, the princess
dashed into her chambers.

At the terrible news, the king summoned all his magicians and wise
men. But try as they might, they could not lift the spell from the princess.

"It is too strong for our magic," pronounced the magicians.

"It is too powerful for our wisdom," concluded the wise men.

Like a dry wind, word of the princess's
shame spread across the land, but no one
could undo the spell.

That night, as the pale moon moved across a cloudless sky, Muoma the beggar boy slept in his straw hut. Muoma dreamt of the bird. It flew overhead, dropping seeds. Other birds fluttered about, singing. As they sang, the seeds flourished into emerald green trees filled with fruit. Out of the fruit billowed the most beautiful human hair Muoma had ever seen.

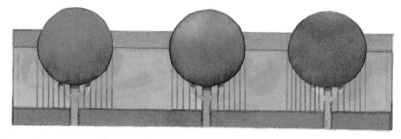

13

The next morning, Muoma appeared
before the king. "If your highness would give
me food and water for a journey," he bowed,
"I will restore your daughter's beauty."

"You, a beggar!" exploded the king.
"What makes you think you will succeed
where others more worthy have failed? Away,
before my anger burns you up like the
desert sun!"

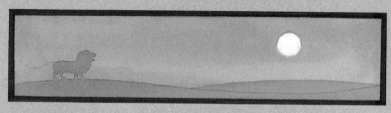

Muoma went home, but late that afternoon he set out from his straw hovel. With a calabash of water and a bag of old boiled beans, he headed towards the sleeping place of the sun on the path he had seen in his dreams. Into the cool of the evening Muoma walked. Hyenas cackled at him from their dens, and Muoma shivered. The roar of a distant lion rumbled through the night, but Muoma walked on.

At last, far behind him, the morning sun emerged over the edge of the world. Still Muoma walked, as the sun climbed through the sky, baking the earth beneath his feet. As he reached the foot of a tall mountain, Muoma sat down on a stone to rest, and to eat a few beans.

Suddenly, a hungry army of ants swarmed around him. "Kindly spare a crumb," groaned their leader. "The drought has left us famished."

Muoma smiled. "I know what it is to be hungry. Here, eat your fill." And he tossed his beans to the ants.

As he lifted his calabash to drink some water, a voice pleaded, "Kindly spare me a drop. The drought has left me scorched."

Muoma looked down in amazement. "A flower? How did you survive the drought? Here, have a drop, brave little flower!"

He rose to leave. Just then a feeble old mouse approached him. "Please, sir," said the mouse. "Please help me search for my children. They are lost up there on the mountain."

Muoma's strength was nearly spent, but he felt pity for the mouse and her children, and he promised to help. With the last of his energy, he clambered up the mountain, his stomach groaning with hunger, and his throat parched with thirst.

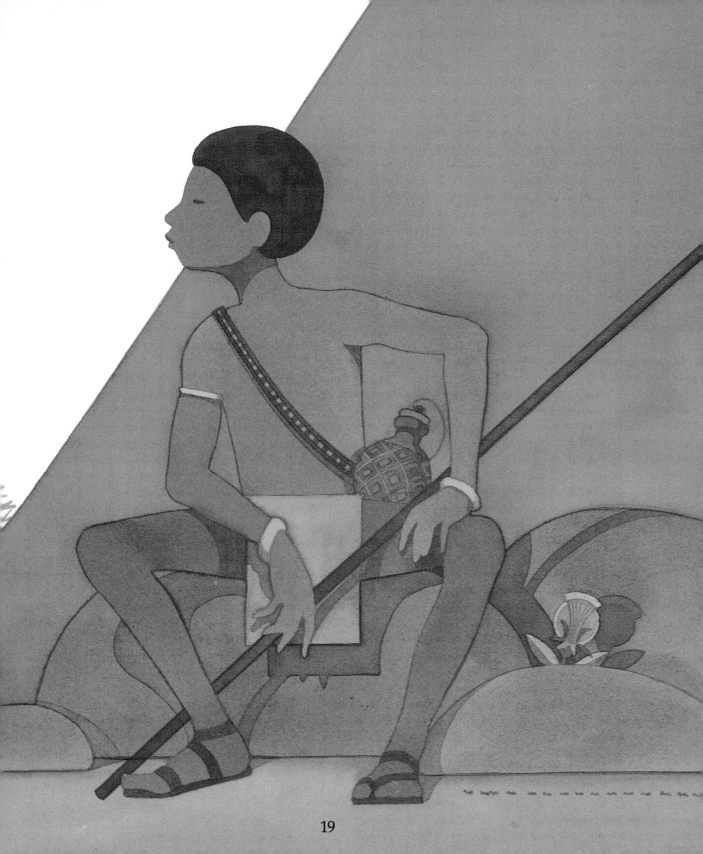

FTER what seemed like an endless climb, Muoma reached the mountain top and came upon a wondrous sight.

There, in a small clearing among the rocks, stood three trees: one of gold, one of silver and the third of emerald green. There was a blinding flash, and the golden tree seemed to burn. As the fire died down, a large bird appeared. It was the bird of Muoma's dreams, noble as a queen and surrounded by a flock of other birds, softly crooning.

At the foot of the silver tree was spread a feast of every imaginable fruit, and pots of cool, clear water. "Be my guest," commanded the bird. "Eat and drink your fill."

Muoma helped himself to a juicy fig, but as he took a bite he remembered. "The mouse!" he cried. Muoma was about to leave to find the mouse and her children when the bird stopped him.

"I know of your promise, for I was the mouse. I was also the ant and the flower. It was a test. To see if you were worthy of your gift."

"What gift?" asked Muoma.

"You came as a beggar, but you have the heart of a kind and generous king," said the bird. "At the foot of the emerald tree is your gift, a seed for the Tree That Grows Hair—the one you saw in your dream. Plant the seed in the vain princess's garden. Tend it carefully, and water it each night. The rest will be up to her."

21

In the time that had passed during Muoma's journey, the drought had bitten deeper into the land. All the king's wealth had gone to buy food and water for his people, and his heart was dry as the sand. The princess, in her grief, had locked herself in her chambers, seeing and speaking to no one.

When he returned, Muoma slipped into the princess's garden late one night, and carefully planted the seed for the Tree That Grows Hair. Each night he crept into the garden to water it. Slowly, the seed pushed forth a tiny emerald green shoot.

One night, the princess opened her shutter. The light of the moon streamed into her chamber. She saw Muoma. Startled, she pulled back into the shadows, watching his moonlit figure kneeling to water the shoot.

The princess watched again the next night, unseen in the shadows. When Muoma had gone, she stole out to the plant and touched its green tendrils in wonder.

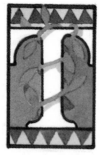HE NEXT NIGHT, Muoma was surprised to find that the plant had already been watered! He looked around, but all was quiet. He felt eyes watching him though, so he pretended to water the plant.

The following night, Muoma crept into the garden and watched from the shadows. Presently, the princess emerged, humming a song she used to sing with her maids. She watered the plant, quietly speaking to it. "I'll tend you to be my companion, for you have no eyes to see my shame." She looked at the dry ground around her. "How beautiful and full of life you are, when all else has turned ugly from the drought."

"As beautiful as you were, and will be yet," spoke Muoma, as he stepped from his hiding place.

The princess started. "Who are you?"

Before he could answer, a gust of wind whipped off the princess's head cloth. "Your hair!" cried Muoma in amazement.

And indeed, the princess's hair was back, longer and more beautiful than ever. Muoma and the princess danced and laughed as he told her of his incredible journey. When Muoma finished, dawn was breaking over the palace wall. Suddenly, the air was filled with song. A massive tree stood where the little plant had been. Birds crooned and danced among its emerald green branches as they built their nests.

"I'll give them some of my soft hair for their homes," laughed the princess, running to get her scissors. "And I'll put it in their nests."

As the last of the nests was lined, the sky darkened. Muoma looked up, past the tree. Thick clouds had spread across the sky, and rain began to fall.

Joy and amazement greeted the princess's recovery and the end of the drought. The king held a great celebration and thanked Muoma. "I treated you as a beggar, but you have proven to be as noble as a great king," he proclaimed. "I would be honored to have you as my son-in-law."

Muoma and the princess were married, and they lived to a wise old age as keepers of the emerald green tree and all the singing birds.

The Akamba people of East Africa live on a high plateau near the equator. If the "long rains" of March to June or the "short rains" of October to December fail to come, crops and animals suffer. So do the people. To people whose lives depend upon the land, weather is very important. They sing and dance about it, and they also write stories about it, like *The Princess Who Lost Her Hair.*

The Akamba land lies east of Kenya's capital city, Nairobi. This is fertile land, just below Mt. Kenya, the second highest mountain in Africa. The Akamba people grow coffee, tea, and sisal. This rich land is also home to great herds of zebra, wildebeest, elephants, giraffes, buffalo, and antelope. Lions, leopards, cheetahs, and hyenas follow the herds.

The Akamba are famous for their carving, especially wood and gourds. A calabash is a large gourd that grows on a vine. It has a tough, outer shell and looks like a squash or a pumpkin. Akamba artists hollow out calabashes and carve the outsides with beautiful designs. Calabashes, like the one Muoma carries, are used to hold water and as cooking pots. They are also used as musical instruments. Calabashes are sold as pieces of art all over the world.

In Akamba stories, heroes like Muoma remind people that every living thing is important, that even the smallest ant, or bird, or green sprout makes the world a better place.